AND THE FORCES OF EVIL

BY J. L. SMITH

The Abominators

The Abominators in the Wild

The Abominators and the Forces of Evil

The ABOMINATORS
AND THE FORCES OF EVIL

The REVENGE of my Panty Wanty Woos!

J. L. SMITH

ILLUSTRATED BY SAM HEARN

LITTLE, BROWN BOOKS FOR YOUNG READERS
lbkids.co.uk

LITTLE, BROWN BOOKS FOR YOUNG READERS

First published in Great Britain in 2013 by Little, Brown Books for Young Readers

ISBN 978-1-907411-64-9

Typeset in Golden Cockerel by M Rules
Printed and bound in Great Britain by
Clays Ltd, St Ives plc

Papers used by LBYR are from well-managed forests
and other responsible sources.

MIX
Paper from
responsible sources
FSC® C104740

Little, Brown Books for Young Readers
An imprint of
Little, Brown Book Group
100 Victoria Embankment
London EC4Y 0DY

An Hachette UK Company
www.hachette.co.uk

www.lbkids.co.uk

For Jimmy Russell, who told the best stories of all

It was a cool autumnal morning at Grimely East Primary School. Which was not surprising, since it was autumn. Children were running just for the sake of it, or skipping. Or jumping. Or kicking piles of leaves around for fun.

But there were five Year 6 children who were not running or skipping or jumping or kicking piles of leaves around like the rest. They were lurking together, as usual, by the bike sheds.

These were the Abominators, Grimely East Primary School's most mischievous children. The ones who played pranks, caused mayhem and whose behaviour made their teacher Mr Coleman sometimes wake up in the middle of the night shouting, "Mummy! Help me!"

There was their leader, Mucker, whose ambition was to be a magician. He had the best ideas – like covering the handle of the kettle in the staffroom with butter;

or fastening a sign saying "DANGEROUS ESCAPED CONVICT" onto the back of the head teacher's car; or scattering cress seeds in the showers on a Friday to see what happened by Monday.

Then there was Cheesy, a pointy-chinned, round-eared boy who loved being in the noisy gang at school because his family at home was so quiet.

There was Bob, a tall girl with a long ponytail who hated the colour pink and flowers, scowled a lot and was brilliant at running.

There was Boogster, who was famous for being able to flick a bogey the length of the classroom, and sometimes further, if the window was open.

And finally, there was Cecil Trumpington-Potts. After his father, Lord Trumpington-Potts, had lost the family fortune *and* Trumpington

Manor, they'd moved to Grimely and were learning to live like normal people.

Cecil had joined the school the previous term, and had surprised the Abominators with his daring exploits and by never, ever giving up.

So, despite the fact that Cecil:

* talked in embarrassing baby talk
* wore outrageous silk pants which he called his "panty wanty woos"
* had a mandolin-playing father who happened to have the longest beard in England, and
* lived in a tiny bedsit, eating mostly baked beans and radishes . . .

despite ALL OF THIS, he had somehow

been (very grudgingly) accepted as an associate member of the Abominators, and as a result was now officially the happiest boy in all of Grimely.

"So, what are we doing?" asked Bob, casually doing a handstand against the bike shed, not at all worried that her ponytail was trailing in the mud.

"What we discussed – Operation 'Spook Mr Coleman'," replied Mucker, out of the corner of his mouth.

"Remember the plan?" added Cheesy. "We do everything he tells us and sit staring like zombies."

"Why are we doing it?" asked Cecil.

"We don't need a reason, you nitwit!" said Boogster, as if it was obvious. "We're doing it for *fun*."

"Ah!" said Cecil. "Fun! I like fun! Cecil's the name, fun's the game! Fun! Fun! Fun! Hurrah for fun! If there's fun to be had, you can count on me – I'll be there!" To show how much he loved fun, Cecil jumped in the air several times, twirling around like a mad ballerina.

"All right," said Mucker, who still got embarrassed by Cecil's very uncool behaviour, "we get the idea. Come on, the bell's gone!"

They filed into the classroom and took their places in the back row. As agreed, they stared ahead like zombies, and were unusually quiet.

It did not take Mr Coleman long to get suspicious; it was very unlike the Abominators to sit so still, and so silently. It seemed somehow . . . sinister. He decided that they must be planning something major. He hoped it would not involve a stink bomb. Or a mouse. Or spiders. He hated spiders.

"I have an important announcement to make," he said, looking above him in case there was something suspended from the ceiling and about to fall on his head. "From now on, you are to have a proper PE teacher, instead of just running round the playground every afternoon.

"We have been lucky enough to have one of the best PE teachers in Grimelyshire offer his services for free to our school. His name is Mr Tuffman. A long time ago, he was in the Olympic javelin team!"

There was a murmur of excitement from the class.

Mr Coleman looked over at the Abominators, who did not react at all. They were still sitting like statues, staring straight ahead. He broke out in a sweat.

"Now, would you please turn to page twenty-three of your maths books, and do exercise four."

The Abominators opened their maths books, picked up their pencils and started to work. Like evil child robots.

Mr Coleman felt his pulse beginning to race. What did they have planned? He was sure that it was spiders. Lots of tiny ones, which would swarm up his trousers. Or perhaps one giant one, ready to leap out at him from somewhere. Enormous and hairy. With red eyes and fangs.

Feeling faint, Mr Coleman sat down. He turned to page twenty-three of his own maths book, his hands trembling slightly. He looked at the Abominators. They sat in a row, heads bowed, writing in their exercise books like perfect children.

It was unbearable. He was so worked up he did not hear the door opening behind him, or the person who entered the room clearing her throat.

"WHAT ARE YOU DOING?" he suddenly cried, leaping to his feet and pointing at the Abominators.

"Excuse me?"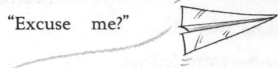

said Mucker politely, putting down his pencil.

"Yes, you five! Sitting there all quiet and well-behaved in the back row!"

"Is there a problem, sir? We don't understand what you're talking about," said Boogster. "We're just trying to do the maths exercise you asked us to do."

"Well, I don't like it!" said Mr Coleman. "You're sitting there, doing your work, behaving perfectly. I DON'T LIKE IT ONE BIT! STOP IT!"

It was then that he realised that there was somebody standing behind him.

He turned around.

It was the Year 5 teacher, Miss Jeffries.

"Mr Coleman, are you all right?" she asked in her kind, melodious voice.

This was too much for Mr Coleman. For Miss Jeffries, whom he secretly wanted to marry, to see him like this was more than he could bear. "I think," said Mr Coleman, in a sad sort of a voice, "that I might need to go on a little holiday. Just for a while."

At which point a paper aeroplane flew through

the air and hit him squarely in the middle of his forehead.

The Abominators were not being zombies any more.

In the headmaster's study, Mr Nutter was pacing up and down. The school secretary, Mrs Magpie, was looking seriously worried. She did not like it when Mr Nutter paced up and down because it usually meant he had a Big Idea.

This always meant more work (which she did not enjoy at all) and not as much time for drinking cups of tea and staring out of the window (which she preferred).

"This is going to be *our* year, Mrs Magpie," Mr Nutter said grandly. "I can feel it. This is going to be the year when we do it."

"Do *what?*" asked Mrs Magpie with a sigh, wishing she could go and boil the kettle instead of having to listen to the head teacher talking nonsense.

"This," said Mr Nutter, "is the year that we are going to beat Lofty Heights Primary School in the Grimely Cardboard Box Festival running-in-a-cardboard-box race!"

Every autumn, Grimely held its annual Cardboard Box Festival to celebrate the day in history when the first cardboard box was manufactured in Grimely's cardboard box factory. The running-in-a-cardboard-box race was the main event, and every year the local schools selected their fastest pupils to compete alongside – and usually beat – the grown-ups.

"But nobody has ever beaten Lofty Heights Primary in the Grimely Cardboard Box Festival running-in-a-cardboard-box race, not since the competition began!" protested Mrs Magpie, her eyes round with surprise.

"This time it's going to be different," said Mr Nutter. "This time we have a secret weapon!"

Mr Nutter smiled at the thought of wiping the grin off the face of the smug head teacher, Mr Butter, from the rival school up the hill.

"And what's this secret weapon?" asked Mrs Magpie.

"Not *what*," said Mr Nutter, "but *who*. Cecil Trumpington-Potts!"

Meanwhile, unaware of Mr Nutter's great plans, the pupils of Year 6 were getting ready for their first ever proper PE lesson.

To the rest of the gang's horror, Cecil had no hesitation in stripping down to his panty wanty woos in the boys' changing rooms. On this particular day they were bright purple.

"Cecil!" warned Cheesy. "Get your PE kit

on double quick, you noodle. Your pants are *not cool*; everybody's laughing at you."

Cecil looked surprised. "My panty wanty woos? *Not cool?* I've never heard anything so silly. They are my proudest possessions. I have hundreds of pairs, in every colour of the rainbow. They are woven from the finest silk from the Far East. Do you know how many

silkworms it took to make just one pair of them?"

"How many?" asked Mucker.

"I don't know," said Cecil. "That's why I was asking you. I should think quite a lot, though."

Boogster shook his head. "They're girls' pants, Cecil. Face up to it."

Cecil looked puzzled. "Well, if they are girls' pants, what do boys wear?"

Mucker whipped off his school trousers. "Boxer shorts! Or just normal pants, like Cheesy's. That's what proper boys wear! Not princess panties like *you've* got on."

There was a long silence. Cecil squinted at his classmates' various pants and boxer shorts without enthusiasm. "Well, I think they're rubbish," he said at last. "They are the most boring colours I've ever seen, and they *don't* look comfortable. I will keep my panty wanty woos, thank you very much!"

The new PE teacher, Mr Tuffman, was waiting for them in the empty field beside the playground. It had never been used as an athletics field before and it had taken all morning for Mr Tuffman to cut the grass and mark out the running track. He was in a very bad mood indeed.

Mr Tuffman was a massive man who had a completely square head. His hair was cut close to his scalp, and his face was weather-beaten and red. Wearing a military style shirt and trousers, he looked more like a sergeant major than a PE teacher.

"Atten*tion!*" he shouted. They all found themselves standing to attention and feeling scared: he did look slightly like a lunatic.

"Quick march, follow me!" he bellowed, setting off across the field, swinging his arms. "Move it! Do you want to be the *weakest*? Do you want to be the slowest in the herd, the wildebeest that gets picked off by the lions, and torn limb from limb?"

"NO, *SIR!*" shouted Cecil, as he marched along directly behind Mr Tuffman, swinging his arms madly. "I most certainly do NOT want to be torn limb from limb by a nasty old pack of sharp-toothed lions. That would be HORRID!"

MARCH!

MARCH!

MARCH

Mr Tuffman slowed his pace slightly, and surveyed the small and skinny child who was marching determinedly along. "That's the right attitude, boy!" he said. "We could do with a few more soldiers . . . I mean athletes . . . with your spirit. I look forward to seeing your skills on the sports field."

"And I look forward to demonstrating them, SIR!" barked Cecil.

"First the javelin!" hollered Mr Tuffman, although he was standing only a few feet away from the children. "A lethal weapon. In my time as a coach and athlete, I've witnessed many horrible javelin-related accidents – one boy got one right through his head. They couldn't remove it. It's still there, which makes getting on trains very difficult for him. Now, line up and have a go."

Boys and girls took turns throwing, with Mr Tuffman commenting on their puny efforts: "Rubbish!" and "That wouldn't kill a hamster!" or "You can do better than that!"

Then it was Cecil's turn. He gripped the javelin and hurled it as far as he could. Which was very far indeed.

"Incredible!" Mr Tuffman was astonished. "I've never seen a boy your age throw a javelin that distance! What is your name and where did you learn to do that?"

"Well," said Cecil. "My name is Cecil Trumpington-Potts and I used to pretend to hunt in the woods using a great big sharp stick. I didn't catch anything, but I threw it LOTS. Sometimes that's all I'd do, all day."

"Did you run when you were pretending

to hunt?" Mr Tuffman was interested.

"Oh, yes," said Cecil. "I'd run after the rabbits, for miles and miles."

"Let's go to the track," said Mr Tuffman. "I'd like to see you run the 1500 metres."

Mr Tuffman blew his whistle and the children set off, most of them at a normal pace, some slightly faster. Cecil set off at a sprint.

"Pace yourself, boy!" shouted Mr Tuffman. "It's not the 100 metres – you'll run out of steam in a couple of minutes!"

But Cecil paid no attention and carried on sprinting until he was lapping the slower runners. As he crossed the finish line, far ahead, Mr Tuffman stared at his stopwatch in disbelief. "This *can't* be right," he said to himself. "If it is ... this is incredible!"

Cecil carried on running.

"You can stop now!" Mr Tuffman shouted. "You've finished the race."

"Do I have to?" shouted Cecil in reply.

When he had at last persuaded Cecil to stop, Mr Tuffman said, "Are you aware that – according to the time you set today – you could be one of the fastest runners of your age in the whole country?"

"No," said Cecil. "I thought I was slow because I couldn't catch the rabbits!"

"You are a natural athlete, Cecil," said Mr Tuffman. "And to think that *I* discovered you!"

"I don't think you did, sir" said Cecil. "I discovered myself years ago! When I saw myself in a mirror for the first time, I remember thinking, 'Who is that extremely handsome-looking boy?' and then I realised that it was *me*! What a great day that was!"

"We shall have to enter you in the

Grimelyshire Schools Olympics and after that . . . perhaps national competitions. This could be the start of something big!"

"I CAN'T WAIT!" said Cecil, jumping up and down in his usual frog-like manner and waving his arms. "I am going to beat everybody else in THE WHOLE WORLD! AT EVERYTHING! I AM *INVINCIBLE*!"

Mucker and the rest of the Abominators looked on in disbelief. Bob, who had come second in the race, was not looking at all happy.

"Guess you're not the fastest runner in our year any more, Bob," said Cheesy, "though I suppose you're still the fastest girl."

"Don't talk to

me! And don't let that Panty-Wanty-Weirdo anywhere near me if he wants to stay in one piece," spat Bob, stomping off towards the school with an angry face.

3

"Is something wrong?" said Cecil, walking up to the gang.

"Bob hates you," said Mucker, "cos you beat her at running. No big deal."

Cecil looked puzzled.

"She hates me? Because I beat her at running? But I beat you all! Does everybody hate me, then?"

"Nah," said Boogster, as they walked back to the changing rooms.

Cecil trotted beside him, looking thoughtful. Then his frown changed to a smile, which changed to a huge grin. He nodded to himself. "I think she loves me," he said.

Mucker, who was behind Cecil and Boogster, burst out laughing. Boogster joined in, and they laughed more and more, until they were wiping tears from their eyes.

"What's so funny?" said Cecil, innocently. "People fall in love all the time, so I hear. And I don't see why someone wouldn't fall in love with me."

"But what makes you think *Bob* loves you?" Mucker finally managed. "I mean, she's just called you a 'Panty-Wanty-Weirdo'."

Cecil appeared unperturbed by the insult. "When girls act strangely towards you and say that they hate you, it sometimes means they actually love you," he said, as if it was obvious.

"It happens in Shakespeare plays all the time. *That's* why she is being odd about me winning the race. She probably wants to marry me. How do you think Lady Bob Trumpington-Potts sounds as a name?"

"It sounds really, *really* wrong, in all sorts of ways," said Cheesy, "and I don't think she loves you – I think she's just a rubbish loser."

"Believe me, she loves me," said Cecil, looking very pleased with himself. "And who can blame her? After all, I possess the most magnificent collection of panty wanty woos in the world, and I wear them with style and dignity. It's enough to turn anybody's head."

Mr Nutter summoned Mr Tuffman to his office, immediately after the Year 6 PE lesson.

"Well," he said, being careful to close the door to keep the conversation private. "What do you think?"

Mr Tuffman nodded his large square head. "I have never in my career come across any child like Cecil Trumpington-Potts," he said. "He is a sporting genius. He seems to have unlimited energy and incredible natural skills. I can see why you wrote to the Sports Council about him."

Mr Nutter smiled. "Yes," he said. "Since he

started playing for the school football team, I have noticed that Trumpington-Potts is an unusually fast runner, so I thought that I should let people know. But I was very surprised that there was such a quick response, and that you were able to offer your services to us free of charge."

"I am happy to help," said Mr Tuffman. "It is a privilege to have the opportunity to work with talented young athletes like Cecil."

"With your help," said Mr Nutter, with a dreamy smile on his face, "we can finally beat Lofty Heights Primary School at the Grimely Cardboard Box Festival running-in-a-cardboard-box race – and then, if his father agrees, you can take Trumpington-Potts to your Academy of Sporting Excellence where he will get the opportunities he deserves."

The two men shook hands, and then Mr Tuffman walked out of Mr Nutter's office.

He walked down the stairs.

And across the playground.

And to the other side of the playing field, until he was sure that he was out of earshot of everybody.

Then he began to laugh. The loudest, scariest, most chilling evil laugh ever laughed in Grimelyshire. It went like this: "Mwoooooo-ooooooooooooooooooooooooooah-ha-ha-ha-ha-ha-ha-ha!"

*

At home that night, over dinner, Cecil told his father about his sporting success at school.

"You probably take after your Great Uncle Sibelius," said his father, chewing on a radish thoughtfully.

"Was he an athlete?" asked Cecil, excited.

"Oh, no. In fact, he was slightly strange, even for a Trumpington-Potts. He thought that he was a coat-stand for most of his life. But *once* he ran faster than a tiger."

"Wowee!" Cecil's eyes shone with excitement. "Tigers are fast! What happened? Did he get into the Guinness Book of World Records?"

"Unfortunately not," said his father. "He only outran the tiger for an hour or so, and then he began to tire. It was a very messy business. The magnificent beast gobbled his entire right leg before Grandfather shot it. It broke the old man's heart to kill that tiger, but enough was enough. It had already eaten at least six of the staff. And one of them was the best butler we'd ever had. It's not easy to find a really good butler, you know."

"How was your day, Father?" asked Cecil, noticing that his father seemed in particularly good humour.

"Excellent," said Lord Trumpington-Potts. "I went to the Job Centre but as usual they said they had nothing suitable for me, so I called in on your friend Boogster's father, Charlie. We decided to try our luck performing in

Grimely Town Square at lunchtime. I played the mandolin and he accompanied me on the guitar. People rewarded us with a multitude of coins, which they threw into Charlie's guitar case. We split the proceeds and I found that I had enough to buy these!"

With a flourish, he produced a bag of broken biscuits from under his magnificent long beard.

"Hurrah! What a treat!" cried Cecil, jumping to his feet and dancing around in celebration.

And so Cecil and his father spent another happy evening together in their bedsit that smelt of cabbages, feasting on broken biscuits and marvelling at their good fortune.

That night, Cecil dreamed of the tiger chasing his ancestor around the grounds of Trumpington Manor, and wondered if he could ever run as fast as his Great Uncle Sibelius.

The next morning at school, the Abominators got a shock. When they walked into the classroom it was not Mr Coleman who was waiting for them. Behind the teacher's desk was a very large, very frightening woman.

Her dyed orange hair was piled high upon her head, and her watery blue eyes stared at them in a scary way. Reading glasses attached to a chain rested on the end of her nose. She was dressed in a purple wool suit and wore a set of large pearls beneath her double chin. However, although she was dressed like a lady, she was actually quite manly looking: her arms and legs positively bulged with muscles. On the desk in front of her was an enormous blue handbag, and she was brandishing a blackboard pointer in a threatening sort of a way.

The children sat down, and the Abominators looked at one another. Cheesy noticed that the woman's legs were quite hairy and was about to whisper this to Mucker when – SLAM! – the pointer crashed down on the desk, making them all jump.

"There will be NO TALKING!" the woman shouted. In her high heels she towered over the pupils. "There will be NO MISCHIEF! There will be complete OBEDIENCE AT ALL TIMES!"

Mucker turned and raised his eyebrows at Bob and – SLAM! – the pointer crashed down again.

"There will be NO RAISING OF EYEBROWS! There will be no SIGNALS! When you breathe, you will breathe in a REGULAR manner! Do you understand me?"

There was silence.

NO TALKING.
NO MISCHIEF.
OBEDIENCE.
AT ALL TIMES!

"DO YOU UNDERSTAND ME? You say, 'Yes, teacher'."

More silence.

"DO YOU UNDERSTAND ME?"

"Yes, teacher," the class all said in unison.

"LOUDER!"

"YES, TEACHER!"

The woman smiled a nasty smile, showing yellow pointed crocodile teeth behind her lipsticked lips.

Boogster glanced at the other Abominators, who all looked as terrified as he felt. All except Cecil. Cecil did not look terrified, he looked quite happy – as if this was great entertainment. Boogster wished he felt excited rather than scared.

"My name," the woman said, pacing up and down behind the desk, "is Miss Marchem. I am the replacement teacher. Mr Coleman is on . . . what he is calling his 'holiday'. In the meantime, you will have me. You will now turn to page twenty-four of your maths books and complete *all* of the exercises. You have fifteen minutes. If you are not finished in fifteen minutes you will be PUNISHED."

Everybody turned to their maths books and hurried to do the exercises.

At break time, the Abominators gathered to discuss the new teacher.

"I can't believe her!" said Boogster. "She's like a . . . monster or something!"

"It's your fault," added Bob, glaring at Mucker. "It was your 'Operation Spook Mr Coleman' plan that made him need a rest from us: that's why she's here."

"I didn't mean it to go that far," protested Mucker. "How was I to know they'd send that great gorgon in his place?"

"I like her!" said Cecil. "I especially like her pointy teeth! She must have about a hundred of them."

"Well, you won't say you like her when she decides to eat you," warned Cheesy. "I bet she eats pupils on a regular basis."

"Really?" said Cecil, looking interested. "Is that why she is so very large?"

"Yes, Cecil," Bob said, in her most sarcastic voice. "Miss Marchem's famous for eating pupils. She eats one every Saturday for her lunch, with a bucket of tomato ketchup.  Didn't you know? Haven't you noticed Lucy Gray hasn't turned up for school this week?"

"I thought she was ill," said Cecil, his eyes widening.

"You thought wrong," whispered Bob ominously. "She's not ill. She's *eaten*, that's what she is. She was Miss Marchem's Saturday nosh, with extra fries!"

"Wow!" said Cecil, looking hugely impressed.

After break, the pupils sat in silence, each hoping that Miss Marchem would not fix them with her pale blue eyes and shout at them for breathing too loudly. Only Cecil did not look afraid: he sat watching Miss Marchem with great interest.

"You, boy!" she said, pointing at Cecil. "Are you Trumpington-Potts?"

"Yes, ma'am!" said Cecil, beaming.

"Don't smile like an idiot, boy!" she barked, walking up to his desk. She slapped a sheaf of papers down in front of him.

"Complete this test!" she shouted. "You have twenty minutes!"

"Is nobody else doing the test?" asked Cecil, looking around at his classmates.

Miss Marchem's eyes bulged with anger. She leant down so that her face was very close to Cecil's. He could smell her breath, which stank worse than a dead badger. His eyes watered.

"You NEVER question me!" she hissed, almost spitting with fury. "You do what you are told!"

"Yes, MA'AM!" said Cecil, who still did not look in the least bit scared. He picked up his pencil and began to do the test.

Miss Marchem straightened up. She paced up and down in front of the frightened class, firing sums at them. Whenever a pupil got a sum wrong, she would go up to their desk, bash the desk with her ruler and shout: "Wrong! Wrong! WRONG!" Poor Boogster, who was not good at sums, ended up with an enormous dent in his desk.

"Finished!" sang Cecil, after just ten minutes.

"Already?" questioned Miss Marchem. She took the test from Cecil and returned to her desk. For the next five minutes she marked the test, using an answer sheet she produced from her giant blue handbag.

"Interesting," she said, when she had finished, staring at Cecil as hungrily as a lion might stare at its prey. "Very interesting!"

When he got home, Cecil told his father about Miss Marchem, with her crocodile teeth.

"She eats a child every Saturday," he told him.

"Are you sure?" said Lord Trumpington-Potts, doubtfully.

"Absolutely," said Cecil. "With tomato ketchup and fries."

As they were talking, they could hear shouting in the street outside, and the sound of running feet. Cecil went to the front door and, as he opened it, saw Cheesy approaching, running for his life, followed by a gang of boys. He recognised them as the Lofty Heights Primary boys who always played dirty at football.

When he saw Cecil, Cheesy took his chance and ran inside. Cecil closed the door behind them. They could hear the boys outside.

"We'll be waiting tomorrow," the leader shouted through the door. Cecil remembered him. He was a tall boy with a long, thin face and he was called Cuthbert.

"Are you all right?" asked Cecil.

"Yeah, thanks, I owe you one," panted Cheesy, "They've always picked on me a bit, but it's got much worse since we beat them at football last month. They're such bad losers."

"Come in, come in!" boomed Lord Trumpington-Potts, appearing behind Cecil. "We were just sharing the last of our broken biscuits. There's more  than enough for three!" His eyes twinkled as he smiled kindly at Cheesy. "And if it happens again, and we're not here," he suggested, "there's a spare key hidden under the doormat. Just let yourself in."

"Thank you," said Cheesy, gratefully. He looked around the sparsely furnished bedsit with interest.

"I know what you want to see," said Cecil with a grin. "They're in here!"

Cecil pulled an enormous brown leather suitcase from the corner of the room. "This," he said, opening the case with a flourish, "is the ENTIRE collection!"

Cheesy gasped. He had seen some of Cecil's panty wanty woos before; in fact, he had seen a lot of them on the disastrous school trip earlier that term when Cecil had tied a hundred pairs together to rescue them all from a ravine, saving everybody's lives – or at least their socks. But Cheesy had never seen all of them until now.

Cecil pulled handful after handful of the exquisite monogrammed silk pants out of the case, letting them cascade onto the floor. Every single colour of the rainbow and every shade and tone in between was there.

"Amazing!" said Cheesy, his eyes round with wonder.

Miss Marchem was in a cruel mood the next day, whacking the children's desks with her ruler at random. The only pupil who escaped her bullying was Cecil: for some reason she seemed wary of him. This annoyed Bob, who was still brooding about Cecil beating her in the 1500 metres.

"That pig-stinking, poncy, prattling little pipsqueak! He thinks he's so special," she muttered to herself as she tackled yet another difficult maths problem. "He thinks he's so clever and so good at sport and . . ."

"Talking to yourself?" Miss Marchem appeared from nowhere at Bob's side, brandishing the ruler.

"No, Miss Marchem; I mean, *yes*, Miss Marchem," stuttered Bob.

WHACK! The dreaded ruler slammed onto the desk a centimetre from Bob's hand.

"And what were you saying to yourself?" quizzed Miss Marchem, leaning in towards Bob. Bob could see her yellow pointed teeth and smell her breath, which was so rank, she thought it would probably kill a cactus at twenty metres.

"I was working out the maths problem, Miss Marchem," said Bob, crossing the fingers of her other hand under the desk.

"LIAR!" screamed Miss Marchem.

WHACK! The ruler crashed down again, making Bob jump in fright.

"STOP THAT IMMEDIATELY!" Cecil rushed across the classroom and grabbed Miss Marchem's arm.

"I *beg* your pardon?" hissed Miss Marchem, turning slowly and menacingly towards Cecil.

"I believe that what you are doing is

wrong," announced Cecil, "and it's also not at all nice. Stop, or I will have to report you to the Grimelyshire 'Preventing The Whacking Of Rulers Near Children' Authority. I believe the penalty is three hundred hours of Hugging Therapy."

Miss Marchem visibly shuddered at the idea of 300 hours of hugging therapy, and lowered her ruler. She straightened up and addressed the class.

"Do not think that this means you . . . *children* . . . will be able to do what you want in my class," she said, her eyes shining with rage. "There are many, many ways in which I can make your lives a misery. The next person to misbehave will stay behind and write out 'I am a horrible child and all children are horrible' five thousand times, and if they make even one small mistake they will do it all over again.

I once had a child writing those lines for a month. He used up seventeen pencils!"

At lunch, Bob sat at a different table from the rest of the Abominators, eating her pasta with a face like a thunderstorm.

"What's wrong with her?" asked Cheesy.

"She still loves me," replied Cecil, as he polished off his double helping in record time.

"No, seriously," added Mucker. "You'd think she'd be thanking you for saving her from a thrashing, but instead she's giving us the cold shoulder. It's not on."

"I don't mind," said Cecil. "She'll come around. They always do – at least, they do in Shakespeare plays. They either get married, or die."

"Cecil, you wombat," said Mucker, shaking his head. "We're not in a parping play. We're in Grimely!"

The first lesson after lunch was PE again. Mr Tuffman was waiting for the class in the field, where he had set up a line of archery targets. He handed each of the children a bow and arrows, and divided them all into teams of three. Cecil was with Cheesy and Mucker, while Boogster and Bob were in different teams.

Mr Tuffman demonstrated how the bow and arrows worked by scoring a bullseye.

"The bow and arrow is lethal in the wrong hands," he said with relish, "but I've only accidentally injured twenty-three pupils in the past five years . . . and nobody has actually died."

The class looked worried. All except Cecil, who looked incredibly excited.

"The team who scores the most bullseyes will win these sweets,"

announced Mr Tuffman, holding up an enormous bag.

Cecil's eyes widened. Bob's widened even further. She wasn't allowed sweets at home.

Soon arrows were flying through the air thick and fast. Each team had twelve chances, with each person shooting four arrows. Cheesy got two bullseyes, Mucker one and Cecil got four. They won by one point, and

57

jumped up and down cheering for about five minutes.

Unfortunately, the team they only just beat was Bob's team. Bob looked angrier than ever.

"We're going to share them with you and Boogster," Mucker shouted over to Bob. "It's going to be a proper feast!"

"I don't want your mouldy old sweets," muttered Bob, blinking back angry tears and stomping off towards the changing rooms.

After school, Cheesy and Cecil walked home together, each with their rucksack full of leftover sweets. It was a slight detour for Cecil, but he wanted to make sure the boys from Lofty Heights Primary didn't make any more trouble for his friend.

It was lucky he had thought of it, because

when they were halfway home they rounded a corner to find the boys waiting.

"Hello, Monsieur Le Freak Ears," said Cuthbert, in his whiny, superior voice. "Is this your bodyguard? He's even punier than you are!"

He walked up to Cheesy and pushed him. Sweets fell out of Cheesy's rucksack, scattering all over the pavement.

Cecil walked up to Cuthbert and pushed him back.

Cuthbert was surprised. He had expected them to try to run away, not to stand up to him. "So, you want a fight then?" he said to Cecil, measuring himself against Cecil's small and skinny frame. Being a coward, like most bullies, he only picked fights he thought he would win.

"All right," replied Cecil, "I'll fight you."

The boys in Lofty Heights blazers formed a circle. "Get him! Get him!" they chanted.

Cuthbert swung at Cecil with his right fist. Cecil was too quick, and ducked. Cuthbert swung at Cecil with his left fist. Again Cecil ducked. Cuthbert tried a kick; Cecil dodged it. Then Cuthbert tried another punch, but again he was much too slow for Cecil.

Getting frustrated, Cuthbert threw himself on top of Cecil, prepared to hold the smaller boy down and thump him. But before they touched the ground Cecil had somehow slipped out of his grasp, and before Cuthbert knew it, he was lying on the ground with Cecil's foot on his neck.

"I think I've won," said Cecil, matter-of-factly.

"No, you've not," said Cuthbert. "Come on, everyone get him!"

The gang of boys in blazers ran at Cecil.

Cheesy started to run to help, but one of the boys grabbed him and pushed him into the hedge.

It took Cheesy a few seconds to struggle out of the thick, spiky hedge. He was afraid of what he would find, expecting to see Cecil being beaten to a pulp.

But instead he found Cecil standing, completely unharmed and without one mark on him, smiling happily as he unwrapped a toffee.

The Lofty Heights boys were lying on the ground looking dazed, and clutching their heads. One had a bleeding nose, and Cuthbert had what was soon to be a black eye.

"*How* did you do that?" Cheesy asked Cecil as they walked on, after he had picked up his sweets.

"I didn't do it," said Cecil. "They did it to each other. All that I did was duck at the last minute."

"But . . . how . . . where . . .?" Cheesy could not believe how quick Cecil had been. One minute Cecil had been there, an easy target, and the next he was several metres away, while Cuthbert and his friends head-butted each other.

"Did you know I once had a bodyguard called Gustav?" asked Cecil.

"You might have mentioned him," Cheesy replied, peeling the wrapper from a lemon sherbet.

"Well, he was a martial-arts expert. I suppose he taught me a few tricks." Cecil popped the toffee into his mouth, and chewed with great satisfaction.

"Ah," said Cheesy. "That explains it."

As they walked off, little did Cecil and Cheesy suspect that they were being watched. Mr Tuffman was hiding behind a tree at the top of the road, and had seen the whole incident through his high-powered binoculars.

"Excellent!" Mr Tuffman said to himself in a sinister voice. "*Excellent!*"

Mr Nutter attended Year 6's next PE lesson. He was excited about the upcoming running-in-a-cardboard-box race and wanted to reassure himself about Cecil's speed. Mr Nutter had only the day before seen the headmaster of Lofty Heights Primary looking particularly smug.

"He won't be looking so smug on Saturday!" Mr Nutter said to himself with satisfaction, as he watched Cecil running around the athletics field as fast as a greyhound.

"Now for the 100 metres sprint!" called out Mr Tuffman.

The children lined up. Bob was next to Cecil and had a determined look on her face. She was an excellent sprinter and decided that this would be the race where she would beat Cecil once and for all. After all, she thought, he couldn't be the best at *all* the distances.

For the first ten metres Bob and Cecil were neck and neck, and then Cecil began to pull away. In desperation, Bob pushed herself, and as she lurched forward, she accidentally knocked into Cecil, who tripped and fell. The race continued, and Bob won.

She ran back to see if Cecil was all right, but he was not. He was clutching his ankle.

"Are you OK?" asked Bob.

"I don't think it's broken," said Cecil. "It's probably a bad sprain. Never mind, these things happen. Well done on winning!"

Bob's eyes filled with tears, which was unusual, as she prided herself on never crying. "Oh, Cecil," she said, "it's all my fault!"

"It certainly is!" said the angry voice of Mr Nutter, who was approaching with Mr Tuffman and the rest of the children. "You deliberately tripped him, and now our best athlete is injured just before the running-in-a-cardboard-box race! Detention for a week, and I will be writing a letter to your parents!"

"It was an accident!" protested Bob. But when she looked around the faces of her fellow pupils, and even her friends, she could see that nobody believed her. Nobody except Cecil.

An hour later, Mr Nutter and Cecil were waiting in the Emergency department of Grimelyshire County Hospital. Cecil was wide-eyed as he watched the doctors and nurses rushing around.

"I'm going to be a doctor when I grow up!" announced Cecil. "I will wear a white coat with pens in the pocket and rush around saving lives! I will probably end up as a brain surgeon, fixing people's brains. Sometimes I might swap them around, just for fun.

Imagine if you went in for brain surgery, Mr Nutter, and woke up in the body of an old lady! Wouldn't you be surprised! You would have to wear all her old-lady clothes and go home and live in her old-lady house."

"I don't think I'd like that at all, Cecil," said Mr Nutter, looking worried.

"Then what if I put your brain in the body of a monkey?" suggested Cecil. "You could swing by your arms, eat bananas and live in the zoo!"

"I don't think I'd like that either," said Mr Nutter, "and neither would Mrs Nutter."

"All right," said Cecil. "I promise I won't swap your brain around when I am a brain surgeon."

"Thank you, Cecil." Mr Nutter was relieved. He was beginning to think that the boy was capable of anything, and didn't like the idea of being a monkey. Not one bit.

Cecil had to have his ankle X-rayed, which he found extremely exciting.

"Nothing broken," announced the doctor. "It's just a nasty sprain. Plenty of ice and rest should do the trick."

"Will he be able to run in the running-in-a-cardboard-box race on Saturday?" asked Mr Nutter.

The doctor shook her head. "I would not advise it," she said. "Plenty of rest is what it needs."

As they made their way back to the car, Cecil could see how disappointed Mr Nutter looked. "Don't worry, Mr Nutter," he said, "I can still run. The doctor only said that she wouldn't advise it. She didn't say she would *forbid* it, did she?"

Mr Nutter turned to Cecil and smiled, hope returning to his face. "Cecil," he said, "if anybody can do it, you can! There's only one boy you have to beat – a talented athlete from Lofty Heights Primary called Cuthbert Sneaksbury. He won the race last year."

Cecil nodded to himself, and adjusted the ice pack that was wrapped around his ankle. "Cuthbert. Well, I know what I'm up against," he said, narrowing his eyes.

While Cecil was at the hospital, Bob had a miserable time. None of the other Abominators would talk to her, refusing to believe that Cecil's injury was an accident.

"You've had it in for him for days," said Mucker. "You wouldn't even eat lunch with him – you've been too busy giving him the evils and sulking cos he's faster than you."

Eventually, Bob gave up trying to explain, and wandered down to the athletics field, where she sat in the long grass at the side of the field. She didn't cry, because only silly girls would cry, but she felt very sorry for herself indeed.

Suddenly, she heard two familiar voices: those of Miss Marchem and Mr Tuffman. What was strange was that they were talking as if they knew each other well. Bob lay down in the grass to make sure they wouldn't see her, as she didn't want to get into even more trouble for being somewhere she shouldn't be.

"So Nutter fell for the 'Academy of Sporting Excellence' story," said Miss Marchem.

"That's a relief. And he has no idea that we know each other."

"Absolutely no idea, the fool," said the voice of Mr Tuffman. "It was a bit of luck that we could get you in here, too. On the spot, as it were! Yes, it's all going exactly to plan. Trumpington-Potts is the ideal candidate for our Secret Evil Forces Military Academy.

He's physically and mentally superior, and although the boy is strong-willed I think he will be unable to resist our advanced and very powerful brainwashing techniques. Imagine using his talents for our ends, to spread fear and destruction throughout the world! He will be an excellent killing machine!"

Bob couldn't help it: she gave an audible gasp of horror.

"Did you hear something?" asked Mr Tuffman.

Bob heard the voices getting closer, and cowered deeper in the grass, trembling. If they found her now, she dreaded to think what they would do to her. Maybe Miss Marchem would actually eat her, without bothering with the ketchup.

"It's nothing," said Miss Marchem, after a long pause. "Now, we know that Mr Nutter is an imbecile, but what about the father? Will he co-operate?"

"We'll tell him the same lie about it being a great opportunity," said Mr Tuffman. "He'll jump at the chance for his son to have a better life. Parents always do. And when he signs on the dotted line ... the boy will be *ours!*"

Then he gave his chilling evil laugh, and Miss Marchem joined in.

"Mwoooooooooooooooooooooooooooo-ooooah-ha-ha-ha-ha-ha-ha-ha!"

By the time Bob reached the school playground, she was thoroughly out of breath. She ran up to the Abominators, who were hanging out by the bike sheds as usual.

"I've just heard Mr Tuffman and Miss Marchem down at the athletics field!" she gasped. "They're plotting to kidnap Cecil! They're going to tell his dad he has this chance to go to an Academy of Sporting Excellence but it's all a lie – they want to turn him into a killer!"

"Nice try, Bob," said Cheesy, shaking his head. "You'd do anything to stop Cecil being a sporting success, wouldn't you?"

"No!" protested Bob. "Listen, I heard them talking. It's true! We've got to do something, like tie them up and make them confess. Or find their headquarters and break in to get evidence. Or even tell Mr Nutter—"

"Count me out," said Mucker. "I don't believe you, and I don't think Mr Nutter's going to believe you, either. You'll just get another detention."

"But—"

"Forget it," added Boogster. "Cecil's in hospital because of you. You are officially no longer one of the gang!"

Bob stared at them in disbelief. To be

kicked out of the Abominators was the worst thing that could possibly happen to her. Being in the gang was what made her feel special, and what helped her to cope with going home to a mum who kept buying her pink dresses, even though she told her she hated pink, and dresses.

She bit her lip, hard. She was not about to start crying and make a fool of herself. If they didn't want to believe her, fine. She would have to figure out a way of stopping Mr Tuffman and Miss Marchem herself. And as soon as Cecil was back from hospital, she would tell him everything. Maybe *he* would believe her.

Unfortunately Bob didn't get the chance to speak to Cecil that day, because Mr Nutter took him straight home.

"You need to get as much rest as possible if you're to have a chance in the running-in-a-cardboard-box race on Saturday. So you're to stay at home and rest your ankle for the next few days. You will have to lie on your sofa and watch TV, and your father will have to apply ice packs straight from the freezer to your swollen ankle."

"That sounds like a good plan, Mr Nutter," said Cecil, "except there are three problems with it."

"And what are they?" asked Mr Nutter, puzzled.

"Well, we don't have a sofa. And we don't have a TV. And we don't have a freezer. Apart from that, the plan's perfect!"

Mr Nutter was surprised when he saw the tiny bedsit in which Cecil and his father lived. He had known they were poor, but he had not realised they were this poor. He sat on the one chair, while Cecil and his father perched on wooden crates. Mr Nutter accepted the cup of tea Lord Trumpington-Potts made for him and even had a couple of broken biscuits, as he was hungry from the afternoon at the hospital.

"Your son is determined to run in the running-in-a-cardboard-box race on Saturday, despite his sprained ankle," he said to Lord Trumpington-Potts.

"I'm not surprised," said Lord Trumpington-Potts. "The Trumpington-Pottses do not let the small matter of injuries get in the way. Cecil's Great Aunt Violet won the long jump in the Olympic Games despite losing her left arm the day before."

"How did she lose her arm, Father?" asked Cecil.

"Trying to pull her brother, your Great Uncle Sibelius, from the jaws of the tiger," explained Lord Trumpington Potts. "But she was not a woman to let the loss of a limb get in the way of sporting achievement. A true Trumpington-Potts."

"That's incredible!" said Mr Nutter. "And it's because of Cecil's outstanding sporting ability that I'd like to talk to you now. Our new PE teacher, Mr Tuffman, thinks that Cecil is an ideal candidate for the Academy of Sporting Excellence. It's a school that not only develops elite athletes to a level where they can compete internationally; it also offers the best academic education in the country. Our school, I'm afraid, is not enough for a boy like your son. I would recommend that you take the full scholarship that Mr Tuffman is offering."

"How wonderful!" Lord Trumpington-Potts

jumped up with excitement. "Where is this school? I suppose we shall have to move house if it's at the other end of the country."

"That would probably not be necessary," said Mr Nutter. "You see, the Academy of Sporting Excellence is a boarding school."

Cecil shook his head. "Then I'm *not going*!" he announced.

"Cecil, you can't turn down such an opportunity," reasoned his father. "We would see each other in the holidays. Think of what you could achieve!"

"No!" said Cecil.

"I suppose I'd better go," said Mr Nutter, getting up.

"Don't worry," said Lord Trumpington-Potts, at the front door. "I'll talk to him. I'll make him see sense."

*

That night, over baked beans and radishes, Lord Trumpington-Potts appealed once more to Cecil. "I want you to reach your potential, like your Great Aunt Violet," he said, "and this Academy could be your chance."

"Father," said Cecil, putting down his knife and fork, "for most of my life I hardly saw you. You were away on camel-riding expeditions. You didn't even know my name. But now we see each other every day, and I've never been happier. I don't want to go back to how it was before. Please, Father."

Lord Trumpington-Potts cleared his throat and blew his nose with one of his fine linen handkerchiefs. He felt very moved by Cecil's words. "Then I will come with you," he said.

"But how?"

"I will get a job at the school, under an

assumed name. I will do anything – wash up in the kitchens if need be. But I promise I won't leave you."

"But, Father," protested Cecil again. "If you worked in the kitchens, they'd make you wear a . . . *beard net*! Would you really do that for me?"

Lord Trumpington-Potts put his hand on Cecil's shoulder and spoke, his voice charged with emotion. "Yes, Cecil, I would do that for you."

The next morning there was a loud knocking on the door of the bedsit.

"Delivery for Trumpington-Potts!" shouted a man in overalls, who was holding a clipboard. And into the bedsit came:

86

* A fridge-freezer
* A comfortable sofa
* And an enormous television.

When Mr Nutter called in to see how Cecil was doing, Lord Trumpington-Potts pointed to the new things.

"We cannot accept these gifts, Mr Nutter," he said. "It is not the Trumpington-Potts way. You should never have sent them. I know you want Cecil to win the race, but this is too much!"

Mr Nutter was confused. "But I didn't send them!" he protested.

"How strange," said Cecil. "Somebody else wants me to win the race. I wonder who?"

"Well," said Lord Trumpington-Potts, reluctantly. "If we don't know who sent them, we can't return them, can we?"

*

Cecil and his father spent most of the next two days and nights sitting on the sofa, watching the enormous television while Cecil's ankle recovered.

They watched programmes about people building houses, buying houses, moving house, selling antiques, going to hospital, losing weight, holding dinner parties for each other, going to airports and nearly missing flights, being rescued from the tops of mountains and learning to drive.

They watched dramas about doctors and nurses, and policemen, and firemen, and detectives.

They watched soap operas where people shouted at each other a lot and cried.

They watched comedies about people living in America, and going to coffee shops. And comedies about people living in England and arguing in kitchens.

They watched quiz shows, and game shows, and shows where people had to jump off things or get fired out of cannons.

They watched until their eyes were large and square.

Then Lord Trumpington-Potts switched off the giant television. "I think that's quite enough for this year," he said. And because Cecil's ankle was now almost better, they spent the rest of the evening playing "Hide the Tin Opener", which was much more enjoyable.

The next day was Saturday, the long-awaited day of the annual Grimely Cardboard Box Festival running-in-a-cardboard-box race.

The entire town was decorated with cardboard boxes of every size and type. They hung from the lampposts, they were piled in giant cardboard-box pyramids, while the rarest and most unusual were on special plinths, illuminated by spotlights. Many of the townsfolk were wearing cardboard boxes, which made getting down the street slightly challenging.

Early in the morning, Mr Nutter turned up at Cecil's door, ready to escort his pupil to the race. "I saw that friend of yours, the girl with the ponytail, hanging around your street just now," he told Cecil and his father, "but I sent her away. I told her that I do not want any more injuries. She was talking nonsense about you being kidnapped – she's obviously extremely unbalanced."

Cecil looked thoughtful. He was wearing a special tracksuit and running shoes provided by Mr Tuffman, and looked very much like an elite athlete.

"All you have to do," said Mr Nutter, as they walked to the town centre, "is beat Cuthbert Sneaksbury."

The crowds had already gathered in the town square to watch the start of the race, many of them wearing cardboard boxes and carrying bowls of jelly and custard. Cecil spotted Mucker, Cheesy and Boogster and gave them the thumbs-up. There was no sign of Bob.

The runners all had to run in identical giant boxes, which fitted over their heads. The boxes made running very difficult, which was the main entertainment. Every year, the crowds enjoyed the sight of up-ended runners, their legs waving helplessly in the air. When this happened, according to ancient tradition, the townsfolk were allowed to throw the jelly and custard at them. This, for many of them, was the highlight of their entire year.

Fitted in his cardboard box, Cecil looked across at the other runners. There were about forty of them, of all ages. He spotted last year's winner, Cuthbert, jogging on the spot, his nasty face smiling in anticipation of another triumph.

Cuthbert looked over and saw Cecil. The smile disappeared and was replaced with a look of anger. Cecil noticed that he then gave a special signal to some of his

friends who were standing further down the street.

The Mayor of Grimely stood in his special fur-trimmed cardboard box, and fired the pistol to start the race. They were off!

"Come on, Cecil!" shouted Mr Nutter, who was beyond excited: he was so wound up, his face was bright red.

Cecil charged down the first street pulling clear of the other runners. But when he was halfway down the second street, he suddenly saw a whole lot of marbles rolling onto the road in front of him. That was what Cuthbert had been signalling to his friends about. Cecil leaped and jumped over the marbles and managed to avoid tripping. Some of the runners after him were not so lucky and the crowds cheered as the first ones to fall were showered with jelly and custard. Cecil looked over his shoulder, wondering how Cuthbert would deal with the marbles, and saw that he was nowhere in sight. Puzzled, Cecil shrugged and ran on.

To the cheers of the townsfolk, Cecil positively flew through Grimely, at record speed despite the large cardboard box. It was hard work: his arms were sticking straight out at the sides and he could not take big strides as the box came right down to his knees. This made it hard to balance: no wonder so many people fell over and did not finish, he thought.

Mucker and the gang had run down some side streets and were waiting for him halfway round the course.

"You're in the lead!" shouted Cheesy.

"There's nobody close to you. Just don't fall over!"

Cecil waved awkwardly and ran on.

About three-quarters of the way around the course, Cuthbert's friends had another go at making Cecil fall. As he rounded a corner, two of them jumped out and sprayed him with silly string. But Cecil was too quick for them, and the small amount they managed to get on him fell off as he flew down the street.

The race was in a circular route, so Cecil knew that when he turned the last corner he would be on the home straight, the main street running down to the town square, where the race had begun.

Which was when he got the surprise of his life. Turning the corner, he expected to see a clear run in front of him. But, instead, twenty metres ahead, he saw the unmistakable figure of Cuthbert.

Confused, Cecil picked up speed, trying to catch his rival. Cuthbert's lead decreased to eighteen metres, then fifteen, then ten. By the time they entered the town square to the roar of the crowd, there were only four metres separating them.

With one final desperate push,

Cecil tried to catch him, but he was too late. Cuthbert crossed the finishing line just ahead of Cecil.

Mr Nutter was waiting at the finishing line, and Cecil saw his look of disappointment.

"Never mind, Cecil," Mr Nutter managed. "You tried your best."

"Well done," Lord Trumpington-Potts added. "I think you are one of only two to finish."

Cuthbert turned round and sneered at Cecil. "Better luck next time, loser!" he crowed.

The Mayor of Grimely called Cuthbert up to the special platform to receive the trophy. "Ladies and gentlemen!" he cried, looking out at the jelly-and-custard-splattered crowd, "I am

100

delighted to present the annual Running-In-A-Cardboard-Box Trophy to—"

"STOP!" shouted a voice, as Bob burst through the crowd and bounded onto the platform.

"What is the meaning of this?" said the mayor.

"Ignore her, she's deranged," interrupted Mr Nutter.

"He cheated!" Bob shouted, pointing at Cuthbert and holding up a camera. "I've got evidence. He cut through a side street – I took photos!"

The mayor took the camera from Bob and flicked through the last few pictures taken. Then he looked up, a stern expression on his face. "I hereby disqualify Cuthbert Sneaksbury from the race, and declare this year's champion – Cecil Trumpington-Potts!"

There was an almighty cheer, as many of the townspeople did not like Cuthbert Sneaksbury. As he slunk off the platform, he was pelted with jelly and custard.

Mucker, Cheesy and Boogster jumped up to congratulate Cecil and Bob.

"You're back in the gang!" Mucker told Bob. "It's official!"

Mr Nutter grabbed the trophy from Cecil.

Then he ran up to the headmaster of Lofty Heights, Mr Butter, and waved it in his very surprised and no-longer-so-smug face.

"At last! At last!" he cried to anyone who would listen. "We've beaten Lofty Heights Primary! I'm so happy!"

Eventually, all of the commotion died down. The Abominators discussed every detail of the race, reliving Bob's unmasking of Cuthbert, and Cecil's victory.

Then Bob asked Cecil, "Where's your dad gone?"

"Oh," said Cecil, looking slightly crestfallen. "He's gone to the school with Mr Nutter and Mr Tuffman to sign an agreement for me to go to the Academy of Sporting Excellence. I don't want to go, because it's a boarding school and I'll miss all of you. But Father's so keen and I don't want to disappoint him. Mr Tuffman's drawn up a legal contract of some kind. Father is going to sign it now."

"NO!" yelled Bob. "We've *got to stop him*!"

"I knew you cared," said Cecil to Bob, "but I had no idea you cared so much!"

"It's not an Academy of Sporting Excellence!" shouted Bob, agitatedly. "It's a trap! It's a lie! Mr Tuffman and Miss Marchem, they know each other! I tried to tell you all but you wouldn't listen! They are in some sort of organisation that brainwashes elite athletes so that they can turn them into killers. They called it the Secret Evil Forces Military Academy and they want to spread fear and destruction throughout the world! You've got to believe me!"

"We believe you," said Mucker. "I wish it wasn't true, but we believe you."

"We've got to stop Father from signing the contract!" said Cecil. "We've got to get to the school!"

But ahead of them the street was packed with people dressed up in cardboard boxes, and covered in jelly and custard. They were beginning to link arms: it was going to be almost impossible to get through.

"Look," said Cheesy, "I'm not going straight to the school. I've had an . . . idea. I'll catch you up."

"You can't just run off," protested Mucker, but Cheesy held his hands up.

"Trust me," he said, and disappeared.

The others looked at the crowd blocking their way to the school. The townspeople, having linked arms, were just beginning the jelly-and-custard celebration dance.

"I don't see how we can get through," said Boogster, shaking his head.

Cecil was struggling out of his cardboard box. "It's going to be dangerous," he said. "And this may be our toughest challenge yet. But we're the Abominators! We can do this!"

Bob, Mucker and Boogster nodded.

"We'll follow you, Cecil," said Boogster. "No matter what, we've got your back!"

They all took a deep breath, then plunged into the crowd of jelly-and-custard-covered people.

*

"Ouch!" and "Ow!" and "Watch out!" called the townspeople as the Abominators fought their way through the crowd.

Sometimes they had to push people to one side, sometimes they had to climb over people who were lying on the ground in their cardboard boxes, and sometimes they had to crawl on their stomachs between people's legs. The ground underfoot was slippery with jelly and custard. The noise of the celebrating was deafening. By the time they were halfway across the square, they were exhausted.

"I don't think I can make it! Go on without me!" Bob called out, having just been knocked off her feet by yet another dancing townsperson in their cardboard box.

"No!" cried Cecil, working his way back to Bob, and grabbing her arm. "We'll never leave you behind!"

Mucker and Boogster helped Cecil drag Bob to her feet. But as she struggled to stay upright, an entire jelly hit her in the face. "It's too much!" she said. "I can't do it!"

"Nonsense!" said Cecil. "You're an Abominator!"

With the others' help, Bob staggered on. Then Boogster was drenched with custard and they had to stop to help him wipe it out of his eyes.

"Bob's right," said Mucker, "we'll never make it!"

"Look!" said Cecil. "Look!"

Up ahead, they saw a gap, a glimmer of daylight.

"We did it!" cried Bob, as they pushed their way through the last of the crowd.

They sprinted up the road, using the very last of their strength to get to the school. Then they ran across the playground, in the door and dragged themselves, panting, up the stairs.

"Stop!" shouted Bob, leading the way as they all ran into Mr Nutter's office. "It's a trick. There's no Academy of Sporting Excellence – it's the Secret Evil Forces Military Academy. DON'T SIGN!"

But it was too late. Lord Trumpington-Potts, seated at Mr Nutter's desk, was holding his large peacock-feather quill pen, having just signed the thick contract. Miss Marchem grabbed it from him and shoved it into her giant blue handbag, shutting the clasp with a decisive, and very final, clunk. She grinned, her yellow crocodile teeth glinting.

"What is the meaning of this?" asked Mr Nutter.

"You should have read the small print," said Mr Tuffman. "There are several pages signing over the rest of Cecil's childhood and most of his adult years to our absolute control, legal in any court of law, and there is absolutely nothing that you can do about it."

"But . . . we had an agreement!" spluttered Lord Trumpington-Potts, getting to his feet. "I thought that you were a gentleman!"

"Well, you thought wrong," gloated Mr Tuffman, shaking his large square head. "The Forces of Evil don't do decency!"

"He's all ours," added Miss Marchem, tapping her handbag with her long red fingernails, "and by the time we've finished with him, he will be capable of acts of destruction we can only imagine! Mwooooo-ooooooooooooooooooooooooooooooah-ha-ha-ha-ha-ha-ha-ha!"

Then Mr Tuffman joined in. "Mwoooooo-ooooooooooooooooooooooooooooooah-ha-ha-ha-ha-ha-ha-ha!"

Mr Nutter looked devastated. "I am so sorry," he said to Lord Trumpington-Potts. "I had absolutely no idea."

"That's because you are a dithering dunderclot!" roared Mr Tuffman, triumphantly. "You're all dithering dunderclots! You're as dim as duckweed! Ha!"

Cecil ran to his father. "Father, don't let them take me!" he cried, grabbing Lord

Trumpington-Potts's beard and hanging on for dear life. "Please!"

But Mr Tuffman already had Cecil by the arm, and Miss Marchem grabbed the other. "It's legally binding," Mr Tuffman repeated, "so you're ours now! Say goodbye to your father!"

Lord Trumpington-Potts and the Abominators could only look on, helpless, as Mr Tuffman and Miss Marchem began to march Cecil out of Mr Nutter's office, towards a terrible, lonely future.

Just then, Mr Tuffman stopped in his tracks, and turned his big square head, listening.

Thump! Scrape! Thump! There was a loud noise of something heavy being dragged up the stairs to Mr Nutter's office. *Thump! Scrape!*

Mr Tuffman looked out of the door, and called out in astonishment. "You, boy!" he said.

At which point, Cheesy entered Mr Nutter's office, exhausted and wild-eyed, lugging an enormous brown leather suitcase behind him.

"What on earth!" spluttered Mr Nutter, distressed at yet another surprise. His morning was turning out to be a rollercoaster of emotions, and right now he was feeling extremely tired and confused.

Cheesy opened the suitcase, its ancient hinges creaking. He tipped the case on its side and a rainbow of silk panty wanty woos spilled out, covering the entire floor of Mr Nutter's office. There were pink ones, purple ones, aubergine ones, sky-blue ones, sea-blue ones, forest-green ones, bright orange ones, golden-yellow ones, mauve ones, cerise ones, ultramarine ones, flame-red ones, crimson ones and every hue in between.

They tumbled and tumbled out of the suitcase, the pile on the floor growing until everybody was ankle-deep in panty wanty woos.

Miss Marchem let Cecil's arm go. She picked up a pink pair of panty wanty woos and held them in the air, between finger and thumb. Her face was wrinkled with disgust.

"Are these ... *articles* ... yours?" Mr Tuffman asked Cecil, his eyes bulging.

"They certainly are!" said Cecil, proudly waving the arm which wasn't in Mr Tuffman's vice-like grip. "This is the entire collection. Apart from the pair I'm wearing, of course. My Nanny Drudgy sewed them herself. Every pair has the family crest embroidered on them. It was a labour of love."

There was a long silence. Everybody stared at the huge collection of silk pants in wonder.

Mr Tuffman's face was changing colour – rather as if it was trying to match the many colours of the panty wanty woos. First it went a sickly yellow, then it flooded crimson, and finally it became purple with rage.

"There is no place," he choked, "in the Secret Evil Forces Military Academy for the wearer of GIRLS' PANTS! Even the *girls* in the Secret Evil Forces Military Academy do not wear GIRLS' PANTS!"

Miss Marchem opened her handbag and pulled out the thick contract. Mr Tuffman took it from her and angrily tore it into a thousand pieces.

The Abominators cheered. Lord Trumpington-Potts leapt in the air at the same time as Cecil and they met in a mid-air hug.

Mr Nutter strode up to Mr Tuffman and Miss Marchem. "Leave my office immediately," he barked, "and don't come back! I will NOT have the Forces of Evil at Grimely East Primary School!"

"Well said, my good man!" said Lord Trumpington-Potts.

"Don't worry, we're going," said

Mr Tuffman, as he and Miss Marchem stomped out of Mr Nutter's office, never to return.

"Cheesy," said Cecil, "you're a top-class hero! You saved the day!"

"It was nothing," said Cheesy, looking enormously happy and proud.

"Now everything can go back to normal!" said Cecil.

"Not quite," said Mr Nutter.

"Why?" asked Lord Trumpington-Potts.

"As the winner of the running-in-a-cardboard-box race, Cecil has to lead the rest of the day's festivities. We'd better get back to the town square straight away."

The rest of the day was an enormous party, with lots of dancing around in jelly and custard, lots of throwing jelly and custard, lots of eating jelly and custard and lots of cardboard-box-related games and fun.

Cecil was the champion, but he insisted that the Abominators shared the glory. "After all," he said, "if it wasn't for Bob, I wouldn't have won. And if it wasn't for Cheesy, I wouldn't even be here!"

Mr Coleman turned up in time to join the fun, back from his holiday early thanks to a phone call from Mr Nutter.

"Mr Coleman!" shouted the Abominators, running up to him. "We missed you *so much*!"

Mr Coleman knew that it wasn't him they had missed; it was being able to be badly behaved – he had heard about Miss Marchem from Mr Nutter. But he didn't mind. He was feeling much better after a week in bed with his teddy bear, with his mum bringing him cups of tea.

"Have I missed much? he asked, looking around at the mad cardboard-box party.

"Well, we had a new PE teacher, but he's gone," said Bob.

"And your replacement teacher – she's gone too, and good riddance!" chimed in Boogster.

"And Cecil won the running-in-a-cardboard-box race," added Cheesy.

"And we saved him from the forces of evil and destruction," said Mucker.

"You saved Cecil from the forces of evil and destruction?" asked Mr Coleman. "How on earth did you manage that?"

"With my panty wanty woos, of course!" said Cecil, jumping in the air and doing a perfect pirouette.

"I might have known," said
Mr Coleman, shaking his head.
"I might have known."

About the Author and the Illustrator

J. L. Smith lives in Buckinghamshire, in disguise.

One of J. L. Smith's greatest achievements in life has been to come second in a closely fought chilli-eating contest in Northampton.

J. L. Smith likes playing the spoons, twirling trays of cups and saucers and starting custard pie fights. J. L. Smith is banned from all local coffee shops.

Sam Hearn enjoys hiding under tables to avoid any custard pies accidentally thrown in his direction. He once designed some superhero outfits for J. L. Smith and himself, but they haven't worn them outside yet.

Abominator Post

J. L. Smith would love to hear from you!

You can use the letter over the page,
or write your own.

If you would like to include a drawing,
that would be even better!

J. L. Smith
c/o Little, Brown Book Group
100 Victoria Embankment
London, EC4Y 0DY

Dear J. L. Smith,

My favourite thing about *The Abominators* is:

_____

_____

_____

_____

I am most like this character from *The Abominators*:

_____

_____

_____

Best wishes,

_____

Have you visited lbkids.co.uk?

We have lots of fun Abominators activities there for you to discover!

Turn the page for our
Jumbo Wordsearch . . .

(You can download and print it out
from our site too.)

Can you find this list of words?

Mayhem ✓

Grimely ✓

Cecil ✓

Bath ✓

Boogster ✓

Burp ✓

Panty Wanty Woos ✓

Cheesy ✓

Beard ✓

Bob ✓

Smell ✓

Top Secret ✓

Abominators ✓

Jelly ✓

Joke ✓

Mucker ✓

Gang ✓

School ✓

Clue: words could be forwards, backwards or diagonal!

Jumbo Wordsearch

```
P Z Q B A N O C J O K E M P
H A O A O B L E E N A V U Q
E B N T A O Z C L C B O C O
L O A T Y C G E L R I S K V
O M I T Y D O S Y I C L E M
T I E L H W M N T O D L R L
E N A N R M A Y H E M F B W
R A M O P Q R N E R R G C A
C T G J K F B O T Z N A F L
E O I H C H E E S Y M N H O
S R E F A B A R A L W G I O
P S M E L L R Y T S R O G H
O D Z O P M D L P R U B O C
T Q L A Y L E M I R G A L S
```

Have you read all the Abominators books?

You can find more mischief, mess and mayhem in:

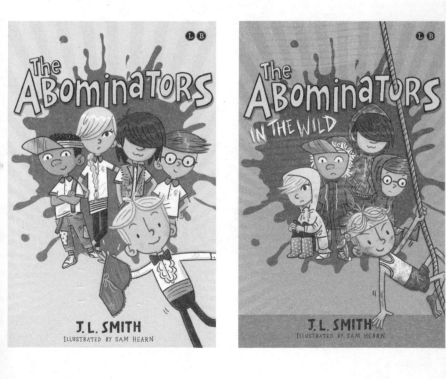